they have orange juice in boston

Genise Aria Reid

they have orange juice in boston

Copyright © 2013 by Genise Aria Reid

ISBN-13: 978-1482533392

ISBN-10: 1482533391

Other Publications by the Author

Devotions for Choristers
(out of print)

How ministers understand and address emotional and sexual
pressures in ministry work
(gradworks.umi.com/34/94/3494888.html)

Glossa Water
(glossagirl.blogspot.com)

Dedication

To our great God, who has no problem creating something out of nothing.

Table of Contents

Chapter One: January 2014

Renee woke up.

It was about 12:30 in the morning. The neighborhood was quiet. No cars, no ambulances. Just a dark quiet night, street lamps shining through the apartment window and onto her bed.

"Why am I wide awake?"

She got up and turned on the radio.

"In local news, the Commissioner's office has confirmed the approval of a ten-year agreement between the state and the Council for Famine Management. The CFM will initiate the first phase of distribution of the AC-cess bracelet to households in the Downstate region. The technology is designed to discourage hoarding by restricting individual purchases of food items…"

Click. Renee turned off the radio. She walked into the living room and sat at the computer.

"I can't believe they bought into this." Renee pulled up to her computer to check her mail. Just as she began typing, her phone rang. Renee ran back into the bedroom and grabbed her cell phone.

"Hello?"

"Hi, sis."

"Ronald! How are you?"

"Well, I'm fine. I'm actually at the subway near your place. I'm sorry to call so late, but can I stop by?"

"Sure!"

"Great. I'll be there soon."

Ronald ended the call and began walking towards her apartment. As he neared the entryway of the building, he saw that the door had been left ajar. He went in without ringing the intercom and rang her doorbell.

Renee opened the door, dressed in a sweatsuit and holding a glass of water. He laughed. "Did I sound thirsty?"

She smiled and put down the glass. "Well, no, *I'm* thirsty… shocked is more like it. I can't even remember when I last saw you. 2011 maybe? Where have you been?"

Ronald gave her a hug as he changed the subject. "I heard that your commissioner signed a little piece of paper."

"Yeah." Renee frowned. "I'll have to leave here soon; I know they won't give me an AC-cess bracelet."

"You don't have to leave that soon." Ronald opened his backpack. "Take a look."

Renee reached into the bag and pulled out five boxes. "What's this?"

"Canned food, dried food, dehydrated. Just add water."

"Ronald, do you have an AC-cess bracelet?"

Silence.

"Ronald? How did you get this stuff?"

"Do you trust me?"

"Of course I trust you. You're in my apartment at one in the morning!"

"That's true. Renee, I need a place to stay for a month or so."

"Are you asking for a referral?"

"I'm asking to stay here. Sis I'm sorry, I'd planned to stay at the backpackers' hostel but when I got there they were full."

"Ronald, you can stay in the guest room, no problem. But there's two things."

"Go on."

"I snore really loud, so you might hear me."

"What's the second thing?"

"You have to tell me where you got this food from."

"Hmm." Ronald rubbed his chin with his hand. "Well, I don't mind if you snore. Are you sure you want the answer to your second question?"

"Yes."

"I'm a food smuggler."

"You're kidding!"

"Shh. Not too loud."

Renee lowered her voice. "When? How did this happen? Who are you working with?"

"I work alone, pretty much."

"I don't believe this. You're no smuggler."

"Renee, sit down."

"I can't!"

"Then stay standing." Ronald took the boxes from her. "Let's talk in the kitchen."

Chapter Two: February 2014

Cathy rolled her eyes. "I'm so tired of going to these stores. Ever since last week's riot they don't have anything in here worth buying. The food is growing fuzz in the packaging! They expect us to eat this?"

Renee looked down. "Yes."

"I'd rather starve."

"You know we can't afford to starve."

Cathy and Renee walked through the store, checking product expiration dates. Most of the shelves appeared to be full: two neatly stacked rows of canned goods, one on top of the other. Renee took a can off the shelf; she and Cathy saw nothing but empty space behind it.

"Renee, there's only ten cans of beets here."

They looked at each other. Cathy pulled two cans of peas. Again, they saw empty space. They walked the rest of the aisle, randomly removing cans and boxes. Same empty space.

"Should we go to the milk aisle?", Cathy asked.

Renee didn't answer. Her lips were turned into a pout, her teeth clenched in an attempt to hold back any noise that would reveal the fear in her heart. *"I refuse to cry,"* she thought.

"Renee? You don't look so good."

An announcement over the loudspeaker cut through the canned music. "Attention customers! We at Price-Rite are committed to easing your transition to the AC-cess bracelet. Simply scan your Price-Rite card at any reading station and one of our associates will help you! Avoid the embarrassment of having ineligible items rescinded at checkout."

Cathy was stunned. "Ineligible items?"

"Remember, don't stand out, stand down! Get your AC-cess bracelet!" The canned music began to waft through the air again. In Renee's ears it sounded like funeral music, a lament mourning the loss of what she thought was a basic right.

"So, we can't get anything," Cathy pined.

"No Cathy. We have to be eligible for something. Lots of people didn't get their bracelets yet."

"You mean chips."

"It's just a bracelet!" Renee's voice got louder. "It's a bracelet. Nothing is implanted."

"Renee, it's the same principle. Can't you see that?"

"No. Let's go to the milk aisle."

They walked to the back of the supermarket and headed towards the corner. Two young children were running and playing as their mother tried to calm them down. As Renee and Cathy got closer, they noticed the line. Eight people, all adults, were waiting. All the milk racks were empty.

A smiling employee walked up to Renee and Cathy, blocking their path. "Welcome to Price-Rite! My name is Jeff, how can I help you?"

"Uh, where's the milk?" Cathy asked.

Jeff, still smiling, launched his memorized response. "The Council for Famine Management has asked all major supermarket chains to remove dairy products from the shelves until the city has completed its AC-cess bracelet distribution. Have you received notification yet from CFM regarding your status?"

"No," Renee replied.

"But I guess *they* have," Cathy added, gesturing to the people on line.

Jeff stopped smiling. "Well, yes. They've had Price-Rite cards for a long time. I think that's why they got their AC-cess bracelets so quickly."

Renee looked at Jeff. "I didn't get anything. No application, no emails."

"Do you have a Price-Rite card?"

Renee reached into her pocket and pulled out her keychain, a small Price-Rite card dangling on the ring. She sighed and looked at Jeff again. He glanced at the bar code, then looked at Cathy.

"Do you also have a card?"

"No, I don't do the card thing. I don't want anyone tracking my purchases."

Jeff handed the keychain back to Renee. "Miss, this series isn't scheduled to get food bracelets until the second phase of CFM."

Renee put her keys back into her pocket. "So what can I get today?"

"Canned goods, boxed goods, and pretty much anything past its prime."

Cathy chimed in. "Like moldy potatoes."

Jeff rubbed his chin. "Yeah, I'm sorry. But we can't break the rules. Well." He sighed, then retrieved his smile. "Thank you." He walked off, disappearing around a corner.

Renee looked into her grocery basket. "I guess I should be happy that I can shop at all."

"Yeah," Cathy agreed. "I mean, the shelves are sparse, but it's not like they're empty."

"Let's get out of here."

They walked to the checkout. The cashier looked at them.

"Is this all you're getting today?"

"Huh?" Renee responded. "Uh, yes, that's all. Times are tight you know."

The cashier nodded. "Oh yeah, I know. They don't even give me discounts and I've worked here for six years with no raise. Well, that's forty dollars and seventy cents."

"Cathy? I just have forty dollars on me."

"Sorry Renee, I only have fifty cents and a Metrocard."

The cashier interjected. "Oh, that's okay. I'll put in the extra twenty cents."

Renee's eyes grew wider. "Wow, thanks."

"It's not really anything special," the cashier said. "Just doing what I can while I can. Okay, forty-fifty from you and twenty cents from me."

"Thank God," Cathy whispered.

"Are you two all right?" The cashier looked at them again, intently. "Will you be able to get by while you wait for your bracelets?"

Renee smiled. "We'll be fine. Thanks for your concern though. And thanks again for helping me out." She and Cathy walked out of the supermarket, disappearing into the crowd of people on the street.

The sidewalks were alive with activity. Seventy or so people stood at the bus stop: not in queue, but not jockeying to be first either. Their faces reflected resignation, as if the classic hustle-and-bustle of city life had been drained from their minds. Another dozen or so people browsed through the sale items displayed in front of a women's apparel store. Sandals for two dollars; shirts for three dollars; jumpers for six. They browsed; no one walked in for a purchase.

"Renee?"

"Mm."

"I don't understand why people aren't rioting."

"Cathy, they did riot."

"But they gave up! One little altercation and the fight is over? New Yorkers don't give up like that."

"Well, welcome to the new New York." Renee pointed at the line of customers waiting to pay their cable bills. "As long as they have a working television and a credit card what is there to riot about?"

They continued walking. Block after block was a portrait of patience, calm, and acceptance. As they neared the subway, Renee paused. "Cathy, do you have another couple of minutes to talk?"

"Actually, I don't. I need to get back uptown. Does it have to be a face-to-face conversation?"

"Yes."

"Okay. I'll try to meet up with you soon, okay?"

"Okay."

"Great. Take care Renee."

"You too, Cathy."

Cathy smiled. "Thanks for the food." She bounded down the subway stairs without looking back, keeping a tight grip on her two shopping bags.

Renee shook her head as Cathy disappeared from view. *"I've got to tell her about Ronald... but what do I say?"*

In a few minutes, Renee was home. She stepped into her apartment, closed and locked the door, and spoke gently. "Ronald? It's just me."

"Renee?"

"Yes."

"You'll never guess what I heard on shortwave."

"Oh Ronald, you're always hearing things."

"I heard they have orange juice in Boston."

Renee looked at Ronald's eyes expecting to see mirth, or some other indication that this was a half-told joke with a punch line soon to follow. He kept talking. "I know it's risky but I want to go up to Boston. Maybe I'll do well up there."

"Don't go there!"

"Renee, I can't hide here forever."

"You're not hiding. You're renting a room."

"Have you told Cathy about me?"

"I haven't told Cathy about you yet. But we can trust her."

"So I've been here six weeks and your good friend doesn't know I exist." Ronald motioned to the couch and Renee sat down. He sat next to her. "Renee, you're a great friend. A real friend. You put yourself at risk letting me stay here. Actually, two risks."

Renee looked away. "The Council," she sighed. "But can't I just say a friend gave me out-of-state food as a gift?"

"What I've given you isn't even supposed to cross county lines, let alone state lines. But I see a bigger problem brewing. You're becoming more than a good friend."

Renee laughed. "You would never go there! I'm almost family."

"Renee, do you remember when we were in graduate school?"

"Of course."

"Do you realize we were never alone back then?"

Renee looked at the ceiling, thinking through the two years of their program. "Wow, I didn't realize that. You're right. We were always in a group; it was never just us."

"I've experienced six weeks of 'just us'."

"No, Ronald. We're like siblings! It's just that we haven't seen each other in a few years."

"I spent too much time joking around," he thought to himself. *"Maybe it's good that she doesn't realize how much I care… it'll give me time to cool off and regroup."* Standing up, he returned to his first point: "Boston is calling me."

Chapter Three: March 2014

Ronald's travel alarm flashed at four in the morning. There was no sound, just an annoying strobe light that switched on and off at irregular intervals. He quickly got up and shut it off.

As he grabbed a change of clothes and headed for the shower, he thought of Renee. *"No,"* he said to himself. *"Gotta move forward."* In his mind he rehearsed and re-rehearsed his trip. *"Get into Chinatown. Get onto a bus. Get out in Boston. Get lost in a sea of tourists".* He smiled. "This should be a good run," he said aloud to his reflection.

By 4:20, Ronald was ready to go. He did a quick inventory of the kitchen pantry: canned tuna, canned salmon, canned vegetables. Boxes of snacks stacked two feet high. Small bottles of water. *"She should be okay for a couple of months,"* he thought.

"Renee?" He knocked on her bedroom door.

"You're leaving now?"

"Yes."

"Okay, I'll be right out."

"I'll be in the kitchen."

Renee stepped into the room a few minutes later, wearing a grey sweatsuit and white sneakers. "I was thinking maybe I could walk with you to the subway," she said.

"Sure. It'll be dawn by a quarter to five."

"I'll be praying for you."

"Let's pray now." Ronald looked down and closed his eyes. Renee did the same as he began to pray aloud. "Lord, You know how I feel…" He paused, then kept praying. "Please watch over Renee and keep her safe. Who better to protect her than You? I thank You that You can do these things for us."

As Ronald continued to pray, Renee wondered: *"Where did he learn to pray like that? He talks to God like he really knows Him. It's like they're good friends, or something… something closer."*

"Amen." Ronald reached for his backpack, then turned to Renee. "Sis? Did you want to pray too?"

"Uh, I think you covered it all." She took a deep breath. "Things might get really bad down here."

"I know. That's why I have to get you food from other regions. You can't starve."

"But Ronald, I'm not the only person here. What about my neighbors?"

Ronald gave Renee a hug. "I wasn't sent here to help your neighbors. My responsibility-"

"Sent? Responsibility?" Renee wondered.

"-is to make sure that you stay relatively healthy." Ronald put on his backpack.

Renee looked at him. "I get the feeling that I shouldn't ask for details."

"You're a beautiful woman, you know. I didn't realize it before now. I mean, before staying here."

"Thank you Ronald."

"I'm sorry. I see how uncomfortable you are."

"It's okay. You're leaving anyway. But what happened?"

Ronald smiled. "Beats me. If I knew what was happening I would have left sooner!" He laughed. "It's okay. We'll be okay."

"Yeah," Renee smiled. "Let's get you out of here." They left the apartment and walked to the subway. As they walked down the stairs, they encountered two armed officials standing at a table.

"Sir?" The taller official looked at Ronald. "We'll have to inspect the contents of your backpack."

"May I ask what for?"

The other official pointed at a newly posted sign. "Yes sir. The Council for Famine Management has asked that law enforcement do random checks in order to ensure that dairy products aren't being transferred between counties, including the counties that comprise New York City."

Ronald opened his backpack and took out all its contents. The taller official picked up a jewelry box. "Sir, I'm sorry but we'll have to open this."

Ronald smiled. "No problem," he replied.

Inside the box was a small, folded piece of paper. Ronald said, "That's a Bible verse a friend gave me years ago. It's very valuable to me: Matthew chapter six, verse twenty."

"Thank you sir, you can re-pack your bag." The officials glanced at Renee. Seeing that she had no bag, they moved off to the side and engaged in small talk while she and Ronald re-packed his bag.

Renee whispered to Ronald. "I won't be able to help Cathy with her grocery shopping anymore."

"Keep helping her. It's just that she can't carry the bags onto the subway. Maybe she can take a taxi."

Renee nodded. "Okay. God be with you Ronald."

"You too Renee."

"How will I know that you've made it there safely?"

"I'll get word to you. I promise." He pushed through the turnstile and hurried downstairs to catch the train.

On the train, he pulled out his small New Testament and tried to read. His thoughts wandered to his travels over the past years. He'd spent six years making contacts in Chicago factories, then two months meeting contacts in New York City, a venture now on hold in favor of his impromptu trek to Boston. *"God, I can't really focus on reading right now. But I thank You for keeping us alive. So far."* Ronald put the small book back in his jacket pocket.

He exited the train at Grand Street and walked up the stairs. Outside, a small group of people were gathered at a storefront depot with small signs affixed to its door and windows:

NYC to Boston $40
NYC to Chicago $70

NO I.D. REQUIRED!!!

Ronald walked up to the window and handed the agent twenty dollars. The man punched a few numbers into his computer, and shortly a one-way ticket printed out.

"Sir? You're not round trip?"

"No thank you."

"Okay." He handed Ronald a postcard and a ticket to Boston. "You want to send a New York City postcard to family? Friend? Enemy?"

Ronald smiled. "Sure. I'll have to think about who to send it to."

His first thought was of Renee. His second thought was of the CFM. *"If I write anyone's address on this card, they'll have an officer at their door before the bus gets to the highway."* Then Ronald realized that his fingerprints were on the postcard. He glanced to his left and right and saw that several of the passengers were filling out postcards and making small talk. Ronald walked back to the window.

"Card? Postcard?"

"I'm not finished yet. I have a question: does the bus make any stops along the way?"

"One stop at 8:30 or so in New Haven."

"Great, thanks."

The sound of brakes cued the passengers: a bus eased its way around the corner and stopped in front of the tiny depot. As the people boarded the bus, several handed their completed postcards to the ticket agent, thanking him. "It's nice to get something for free," one passenger commented.

There were about thirty-five people who boarded the forty-seven seat bus. Ronald walked to the back of the bus and stretched out over two seats. As the bus pulled off and turned the corner, he looked out of the window just in time to see the ticket agent hand the collected postcards to a well-dressed man wearing a CFM patch on his jacket.

Ronald reached into his own jacket, pulling out the unaddressed postcard. *"Maybe I'll mail this to Renee from New Haven."*

Chapter Four: April 2014

Renee looked out of her window to see a delivery truck parked in front of her building. A few seconds later, her intercom rang.

"Hello?"

"Elite Fleet. Delivery."

"Okay, I'll be right out." She put on a pair of sandals and walked to the front of the building, where the driver had a hand truck stacked with several boxes.

"Renee Dupree?"

"Yes, I'm Renee."

"All these are yours."

"Um, do I have to sign anything?"

"No ma'am. I just have to scan them." He scanned each box and put them near the door. "I'm sorry, we're no longer allowed to carry items into customer's homes. I hope you can carry them from here."

Renee smiled. "I'll get it done, thanks."

"Thank you ma'am. Have a nice day."

As the driver left, Renee looked at the return address on the boxes. *"Yale?"* She pushed and dragged the boxes into her living room. Opening the first, she saw packets of powdered milk.

"This has to be from Ronald," she thought. She looked for a note, but found only a postcard with a picture of the New York City skyline. On the back of the postcard was a short note in his handwriting, but no signature:

"I was warned. I turned aside."

She opened the second box: a new sweatshirt and sweatpants. A zip-up spring jacket. All plain, not a logo to be found.

A small box caught her attention. It looked like Ronald's old jewelry box, and it was. Renee opened it and saw two small papers. One, Ronald's, was a well-worn piece of paper with a handwritten Scripture reference: Matthew 6:20. The other paper looked new. Renee unfolded it. It read, "I.O.U. a bracelet. Please keep my jewelry box as collateral until I bring you your own. R."

"But what does he mean?" she wondered. *"An AC-cess bracelet? Some other jewelry?"* Renee put the papers back in the box and laid the box in a kitchen drawer. *"That old box is worth so much to him. Why would he give it to me?"* She went and sat

on her bed, too absorbed in thought to return to the living room.

Chapter Five: May 2014

"Cathy!"

Renee gave her friend a big hug. "My gosh, it's been months."

"Yeah," Cathy echoed. So much going on."

"So what happened to you?"

"I was detained."

"What? What did you do?"

"I was stopped on the street by an agent. They caught me with two gallons of milk I'd brought from the Bronx."

"They stopped you on the street?"

"Yeah, apparently they can do that in Manhattan County now, if they see you with milk. It's coded by borough."

"Thanks for the heads-up."

Cathy nodded. "It'll trickle into Kings County soon. You'd better be careful."

Renee nodded her head. "Got it."

The two friends walked from the subway to Renee's apartment, occasionally glancing up at the newly installed CFM cameras which sat atop the streetlamps.

"Are they on yet?" Cathy asked.

"No. These haven't been activated. I'm not sure why."

They walked into the apartment and Cathy immediately headed for the couch. "That train ride was so exhausting. It's like the Council has taken over everything. I should move."

Renee sat in a chair. "Cathy, listen. I need to talk to you."

"What is it Renee?"

"I've been getting food from Yale."

"Wow, that's cool. Alumni privileges!"

"Cathy, I didn't attend Yale."

"So how did they get your address?"

"They didn't. It's from a guy I know; one of my classmates from when I was in graduate school."

Cathy shook her head. "You need to get out of that arrangement."

"Cathy, it's not like that. We're-"

"Just friends? That how it always starts."

"Never mind." Renee stood up. "So anyway my friend, who is just a friend, sent some powdered milk. And some food." She decided not to mention the clothing.

Cathy sat forward. "Wow, I never thought of getting powdered milk. That's so much easier to take between the counties."

Renee got a piece of paper and a pencil. "Okay, let's try to figure out how to get this food to your home without getting you arrested. Again."

"Excuse me, I was detained. Not arrested."

They strategized for half an hour. Each plan had a glitch. Subways were out of the question: the CFM had officials posted at every station in Manhattan. Mailboxes were too small, and there were rumors that post office workers were supporting the efforts of the CFM. Taxis were safe, but a taxi ride from Renee's to Cathy's was costly; they could do that once a month, maybe twice, but not regularly. The Commissioner's office had even modified the bus routes so that most buses no longer crossed county lines…

Suddenly, they looked at each other.

"The airport buses!" they said in unison.

Cathy continued. "I'm sure they're not doing stop-and-frisk on the tourists."

"I'll pack you a carry-on." Renee walked to the closet and pulled out a small travel bag. "This one has an extra piece to keep the bottom flat, so that should be enough to hide a few things underneath."

"Cool. And I'll put my jacket and scarf in it, just so it doesn't look so empty."

"No, I have clothes to spare. I think we should pack it full like you're really going somewhere, in case they stop you."

After the packing was done, Cathy pulled out her Metrocard and headed for the door, slinging Renee's bag over her shoulder. "Okay. I'll take the Brooklyn bus to the airport, then catch the Manhattan bus out."

"I think that'll work."

"Renee?"

Renee looked at Cathy, waiting for her to continue.

"Thanks for giving me your travel bag. And please tell your friend I said thank you for the food."

"Thank you Cathy. I will."

Cathy headed out the door with a wave. Renee sat back down, her mind reviewing the past few months. *It seems like it's the poorest communities that have lost access to staple foods. Ha ha, AC-*

cess. Very funny. What's the point of having an AC-
cess bracelet if there's nothing to access?"

The phone rang. Renee glanced and saw the area code: 203. She picked up the call.

"Hello?"

"Sis, so good to hear your voice!"

"Ronald?"

"That would be me!"

Renee smiled. "Things don't seem so bad when I hear your voice."

"Whoa, that compliment is kind of pushing the boundary line. You're dressed, aren't you?"

"What?"

"You're dressed."

"Uh, yes." Renee frowned, thinking, *"Was Cathy right?"*

"Great! Come outside please. But stay on the phone."

Renee picked up her keys, leaving the apartment with a very confused look on her face. "Ronald, what's going on?"

"You see the Prius?"

"Oh my God, you're in the city again?"

"No, I'm not in New York at all. I'm at a computer. I have a view from the surveillance cameras."

"That's impossible. My block hasn't been activated yet."

"Is that what they told you, my gullible friend? Keep walking towards that car. I'm on campus, in one of the computer rooms. All the cameras on your block are up and running. But the cameras in the middle of the block have the view obstructed because of the trees. Your county doesn't have the money now to cut back the trees, so they're just going to wait until next spring. Your building entrance won't be visible until the trees lose their leaves in the fall. Now I have to ask you to trust me."

"You and the trust thing! You know I trust you."

"Get into the car. The door's open."

"But Ronald, there's someone in the car."

"Yes. Get in on the passenger side and put me on speakerphone." Renee followed his instructions, and Ronald continued.

"Darren, this is Renee. Renee, meet Darren." They looked at each other and shook hands, Renee managing a weak smile.

"Renee, Darren is my contact person for Gate Beautiful Church of the Savior. He's agreed to look out for you if something should happen to me."

"I'm one of the assistant pastors," Darren added.

"Thanks, thanks to both of you," Renee sighed, "but I'm not sure why you guys are looking out for me."

"Sis," Ronald replied, "It's just the way it is."

Darren turned towards Renee, but spoke to Ronald. "Renee's not wearing an AC-cess bracelet, so I'm assuming she's not going to get one, right?"

Renee answered. "The guy at the supermarket said I was scheduled for Phase Two, in 2015."

"When did you talk to him?" Darren asked.

Renee tilted her head and closed her eyes, trying to remember. "I think that was back in February."

Darren looked down.

"Darren? Ronald?"

Ronald spoke. "Sis, that supermarket probably won't be around that long. Do you still have a supermarket card?"

"Yes, I keep it with my keys."

"Buy all the canned goods that they'll allow you to, and stock them in your apartment."

"But Ronald, this is a neighborhood! Lots of people need to eat."

"I'll talk to you soon Darren. Sis, take me off speakerphone and head back home."

"Okay boss." Darren started his car, the electric-powered engine making virtually no sound at all. "Take care Renee. Good to meet you." As she closed the door, Darren drove off.

"Renee." Ronald spoke with urgency. "You *have* to stock up. Just trust me and do it."

"It's not fair to the people. I feel bad that I have so much."

"Sis, you don't have much. You have enough to get you through six months. That's all."

"That can't be right."

"It's right. Listen, I have to go now but I'll call you again soon. Renee?"

"Yes?"

"Don't feel guilty."

"Okay. Thanks."

"Goodbye my friend."

"Goodbye."

Ronald hung up the phone. He looked around the empty lab: all of the students had gone home at the close of the spring semester, and most of the faculty had gone as well. He turned off the computer, but not before looking at Renee's block one final time. *"I hope I can get her set up for the rest of the year, at least…"*

Ronald walked to the door where his janitor supplies were neatly stacked on a wheeled cart, and continued with his work.

Chapter Six: June 2014

"The Council for Famine Management is reporting that, due to limited gas and oil supplies, delivery of food to urban markets will be reduced fifteen to twenty percent for the months of July and August. CFM Director Blake Stearns and New York State Commissioner Aaron Allston held a joint news conference today, in which they assured the public that there would be minimal disruption-"

Knock-knock-knock. A firm, steady hand rapping on her apartment door jolted Renee. She looked through the peephole and saw two uniforms.

"Yes, who is it?"

"Police, ma'am. We'd like to ask you a few questions."

Renee opened the door, but left the safety latch on. "Yes?"

"We're assisting the Council for Famine Management in locating individuals who may be involved in transporting produce across regions, in violation of CFM code. Have you seen this man?" The officer produced a photo of Ronald, standing by a search table in a subway station.

"I've seen him," Renee replied quickly. "He was in the area a couple of months ago."

"Do you know where he is now?"

"No. But I can see in this picture that his bag was being searched by two of your officers, and I assume that if they had found something they would have detained him."

"Thank you ma'am. Have a good evening."

"Thanks. You too."

The officers left, and Renee took a deep breath. *"It's okay... there's nothing here with his name on it. And they don't have a compelling reason to go after me for anything... I think."*

Renee turned her attention back to the television, which was still broadcasting the evening news.

"... and we are facing our third consecutive year of summer drought, which has drastically affected American corn crops. We expect that prices for other corn-based products will rise an average of seven to ten percent over the next year..."

Click. Renee shut off the television. She picked up Ronald's old jewelry box, talking out loud to herself. "I know. 'Store up for yourselves treasures in heaven.'" She put down the box. "Well, that's

easy enough. There's nothing on earth left to store."
Suddenly, though, Renee realized that she had quite a bit in storage. She could stay home for months without having to go to the supermarket. She could go to Gate Beautiful if she needed help. She could-

CRASH!

The sounds of breaking glass and loud voices were soon followed by the sound of police sirens. Renee retreated further into the apartment, not sure of where the incident was occurring. Reaching for her radio, she found a music station and turned up the volume in an attempt to drown out the outside noise. Instead of soothing her, the music intensified the irony: the playlist sounded like "business as usual," but the past six months had been extremely unusual.

Aware of the irony, she tried to pray. "Lord? Thank You that You're in charge and I don't have to be afraid... but I'm really afraid right now. I wish I had something better to say to You. I mean, something more faithful-sounding. But I don't see how You're going to get us out of this crisis. Why is it so hard to get food? Why is everyone going on like this is normal?"

Abandoning her prayer, Renee shut off the radio and turned the television back on. Intentionally avoiding the news channels, she sat in front of the screen watching movies through the evening and well into the night.

She found herself waking up. *"Wow, I must have been really tired... What time is it?"* In her semi-conscious state, she shut off the television and walked to the bedroom. Remembering the sirens, she whispered another prayer.

"Oh, God, wow. I spent six hours with the TV and not even a minute with You. Is that why Ronald prays like he knows You? Is he spending a lot of time with You?"

Silence.

Chapter Seven: July 2014

Ronald finished packing his bookbag. The small bag held only his jacket, a few hundred dollars, and his pocket-sized Bible. As an afterthought he took the money out of the bag, placed it in the inner zipper pocket of his jacket, then stuffed the jacket back into his bag.

He walked a few blocks from the campus to the New Haven station, where a Metro-North train waited. At the kiosk, he bought a round-trip ticket. He boarded the train, which soon left the station and headed west. A uniformed agent walked through the train car. "Tickets, please. Thank you. Tickets? Tickets please?" As he neared Ronald, Ronald gave him the ticket:

NEW HAVEN TO FORDHAM

"Thank you," the agent said, punching a small hole in the ticket and barely giving Ronald a second glance.

As the train neared New York, Ronald wondered if he should have remained in Connecticut. *"No,"* he said to himself. *"I need to see what's going on in the city."*

Upon reaching his stop, Ronald exited the train and walked quickly onto the campus of Fordham University. He saw a security guard a few feet ahead, and soon caught up with him.

"Sir?" he asked.

The guard stopped. "Yes?"

"Good morning, where are the campus tours?"

"Oh, they start from the Admissions office. Just keep following this path. The next tour starts in a few minutes."

"Thanks."

Ronald reached the tour group and spent the next hour learning the layout of the campus. Strangely, and similar to his experience at Yale, there was no CFM presence anywhere on the campus grounds. As he headed toward the gate that separated Fordham University from Fordham Road, he suddenly remembered that there were no bag-search tables at the Metro-North stations either.

Ronald paused to look up and down Fordham Road. There were dozens of people waiting at the city bus stops in both directions. Across the street from the campus were several armed officers. Ronald glanced further down the block opposite campus and saw two CFM agents checking a young woman's shopping bags.

Not wanting to stay outside for too long, Ronald went back into the station for the return trip to Connecticut.

The lengthy ride gave Ronald plenty of time to think. *"Why is it so easy for me to get supplies in New Haven? Why are there no CFM agents on the college campuses? Why am I able to mail so many things without Elite Fleet asking me any questions?"*

As the train neared New Haven, Ronald got an answer.

"Affluence."

"My God," Ronald whispered.

"There is no 'famine management' for the affluent."

"Yes. I see it now."

Ronald looked out of the window for the last few minutes of the ride, silently wondering whether he should make an effort to move Renee out of the city… or whether it was even appropriate for him to try.

Just as the thought to call her crossed his mind, he received a text message from Darren:

"Council at my Gate. Lay low."

Chapter Eight: August 2014

Renee caught a bus heading east. It was to be her first visit to Gate Beautiful. As she approached the front door, she was greeted by one of the congregants.

"Hello, my name is Sarah. Welcome to Gate Beautiful."

"Thanks, my name is Renee."

They shook hands as Sarah continued talking. "The chapel is right ahead, and the restrooms are down the hall to the right."

"Great, thanks." Renee walked down the hallway. In the women's restroom, she pulled out her cell phone. She had not heard from Ronald since his call three months ago, and she was conflicted. Should she take the chance and call?

She decided to turn off her phone so that she wouldn't be distracted during the service. *"Maybe after church,"* she thought.

As she walked back towards the chapel, Renee saw two clergymen talking in one of the offices.

Though she could not hear the entire conversation, she did catch a phrase: "…when Darren gets back."

"Oh no," Renee thought. *"He must be on vacation. Do all pastors take vacation in August?"*

She was disappointed, but decided to stay for the service anyway. Had she tried to catch a bus back to her own church, she would have arrived too late for her own pastor's sermon.

The service at Gate Beautiful began somewhat predictably. Two hymns, a chorus, a prayer, a creed. After the creed, one of the clergymen walked up to the podium.

"Family, I want to update you on Pastor Darren." The whole church, even the young children who had been fidgeting in the back rows, became very quiet.

"As you may have heard, he was found in contempt for refusing to cooperate in the search for Ronald Lee, his colleague and our friend from Olympia Community Church out in Chicago."

Renee looked down as her heart began racing. The man continued speaking.

"Pastor Darren has already been detained for fourteen days, so we expect he'll be held at the CFM's detention center for perhaps another twenty-six days. Our denomination has informed us that, although our board has requested Darren's reinstatement immediately upon his release, they- that is, the denomination- will not permit Darren to remain in the apartment that is subsidized by our district."

Murmurs began rumbling in the chapel.

"So, Pastor Darren will more likely than not need housing when he's released from detention. To be honest with you, our church can't afford to cover unsubsidized housing unless we cut back on the food pantry, which I know none of us wants to do. So if you could all pray about this… we'll trust God to help Pastor Darren, and help us, as we move on."

Renee tapped the person in front of her. "Excuse me, what's the minister's name who was just speaking?"

"Pastor Joe," the woman answered.

At the close of the service, Renee approached him. "Excuse me, I have a place where Pastor Darren can stay. It's not too far from here."

A few congregants, clustered in the foyer, overheard her. Their reactions were a mixture of joy, surprise, and skepticism. Pastor Joe smiled.

"Well, it seems our prayer has been answered. Let's talk more after I finish greeting everyone."

"Sure." Renee half-smiled and sat down in the lobby, conscious of the stares of a few congregants. *"They're suspicious of me,"* she said to herself.

As she waited, an older woman walked over to her.

"Miss, it doesn't look good for you to be taking in a man."

Renee responded immediately. "I don't believe we've met. My name is Renee Dupree. Good morning."

"Good morning."

"May I ask what your name is?"

"Carol Caine."

"Ms. Caine, I did not say Pastor Darren could live with me. I said I have a place where he can stay. But I'm sure your pastor would appreciate your concern for his reputation."

"I'm very sorry for the misunderstanding."

Renee shook her head and muttered to herself as Carol walked away. *"I don't see anyone else offering to help... let me relax. Maybe none of them are in a position to help."*

The last few congregants exited the building, and Pastor Joe walked across the lobby and sat with Renee.

"I'm Pastor Joe."

"I'm Renee."

"Do you know Darren?"

"I met him once, some months ago."

Pastor Joe looked directly into her eyes. "Renee, do you know Pastor Ronald?"

"I know a Ronald Lee that I went to school with in Chicago, but to my knowledge he's not a pastor."

Joe pointed at the bulletin board. "Let's check. He was a guest speaker here back in 2012. His picture is on the board over there." Joe remained seated as Renee stood up and glanced at several photos. About twenty seconds later, she found him.

"That's Ronald." She turned to Pastor Joe. "Ronald is my friend; we met in graduate school. But he never told me he was a pastor."

"I'm guessing there might be other things he didn't tell you."

"I'm afraid to ask."

Pastor Joe smiled. "Well, anyway, about Pastor Darren. Darren should be released in about a month."

"I have a two bedroom apartment and I'm happy to let him have the whole thing."

"Where would you stay?"

"I have a friend in Manhattan that I can stay with for a month, easily."

"Why not just stay where you are if you have two bedrooms?"

"One of your congregants looked at me like I was a problem."

"Renee, you're willing to inconvenience yourself for a person you don't even know. That is so beautiful."

Renee sighed. "There's things you don't know about me."

"It's okay. You wouldn't have volunteered to help unless you cared. And God will help you with those things you say I don't know about you."

"Thank you," Renee said softly. "Well, if Pastor Darren doesn't mind, he can share the apartment for as long as he needs."

"I'll let him know."

"I'm sorry your denomination isn't supporting him."

"Well, Renee, they're kind of backed into a corner. Technically, Darren's out of compliance, so they have to side with the CFM."

"Shouldn't they side with Jesus?"

They looked at each other as silence rushed in to their conversation. After a long pause, Renee continued. "Staying at my place might make things worse."

"Renee, don't worry. Whether Darren is there or not, God will certainly honor your willingness to help."

"Thanks Pastor Joe." They looked at each other in silence again, sensing the close of their conversation.

"I'll update you soon."

"Can I ask you a question?"

"Sure."

"Why didn't Ronald tell me he's a pastor?"

"Well, he's always worked with numbers. Hardly ever preached. Most people assume that pastors work with people, so he almost never uses that title."

"I understand. Thanks for allowing me to help Pastor Darren."

"Sure. Take care Renee."

The bus ride home was swift. Most of the bus stops had no passengers waiting to board, so the driver glided past. Renee looked out of the window and surveyed the nearly empty streets. *"Is everyone at home? Have that many people moved out of the city? What will the fall and winter bring?"*

"Will I see Ronald again?"

Chapter Nine: September 2014

R-r-r-ring! Renee's house phone rang at three o'clock on a cool Sunday afternoon. She recognized the number on the caller I.D. and hastily picked up the phone. "Pastor Joe?"

"Yes, is this Renee?"

"Yes sir. Good afternoon."

"I hope you're well."

"Yes I am, thanks."

"Well, I'll keep this short. The denomination is transferring Pastor Darren to a different region, so we won't have any housing needs. But thank you again for your generosity and your willingness to serve."

"Oh wow, okay. Um, I hope it works out for him."

"Thank you Renee. You have a good day now."

"You too Pastor Joe. Oh, Pastor Joe?"

"Yes?"

"Do you know where they're sending him?"

"Yes. He'll be in Boston."

*****

The leaves had begun falling in New England. The landscape was awash in reds, oranges, and yellows, and the newly bare branches framed gaps in the landscape. In New Haven, Ronald walked the grounds more slowly than usual. Somehow, he sensed that it would soon be time to leave.

The summer drought and poor corn harvest had affected every sector of work and leisure. There was less food, gas prices were higher, and even the junk food industry was cutting back on the manufacture of chips and candies. The college students noticed the difference immediately, and they began to hoard the snacks they were able to acquire. Ronald was finding it increasingly difficult to send supplies to Renee. He wondered if he should return to Chicago, where he knew he could count on his contacts who worked in the factories there.

For the day, though, his concern was granola bars. The students were aggressively scouring the campus and its surrounding neighborhoods for the same fare non-students were amassing: food packaged in small portions, and pre-packaged meals that only needed water added. The students, too, had caught onto the ease of *Elite Fleet*. Their shipping store near campus, which in previous semesters had only seen moderate lines, now had lines going out of the store and halfway down the block. Students dutifully mailed food home to their struggling parents and siblings.

Ronald found he was expending more time and energy on his food searches. One morning he took a walk to think and pray. He walked into the library and took the escalator one flight up, then walked to one corner of the room. A small velvet rope surrounded a glass case, protecting the fragile Gutenberg Bible inside. Standing as close to the rope as he could, Ronald stared at the open book. *"Oh, I wish I had taken German instead of Chinese,"* he thought to himself. After a few minutes, he left.

Noticing his break was nearly done, he dashed into one of the campus buildings. Surprised to see a row of vending machines missing, he got on his phone to call a co-worker.

"Hello Ron."

"Hi Dan, I'm in Phelps Hall. What happened here?"

"You mean the vending machines?"

"Yes."

"A frat stole them."

"What?"

"Yeah, we have them on the surveillance video. First we thought it was a prank, but it wasn't. They took the snacks and mailed them to their fraternity brothers down in Philadelphia, and the guys down there have been selling the snacks for five bucks a piece."

"What does that mean for us?"

"Nothing. Their parents are hefty donors to the college. The fraternity will stay on campus and none of them will be expelled. We'll have new vending machines in by Friday... more secure, of course."

"Of course."

"Okay Ron. See you in a few minutes."

"See you Dan."

Ronald sighed, praying out loud. "God, I feel like I'm just treading water here." Inside, he felt like he heard an answer:

"It's okay, son. Just a few more months."

Chapter Ten: October 2014

Darren came to learn, quickly, that Boston was not all it was presumed to be. The people were wonderful, and the crisp autumn weather was refreshing, but the rumors of abundance were false.

He walked into a local market on a Saturday morning. The display case that was designed to hold corn stood bare. Underneath, the bins held a few rotting potatoes. An immediately adjacent bin held two half-gallons of unrefrigerated orange juice. Darren picked up one of the containers: it wasn't even half a gallon. The fine print said "52 ounces." He checked the expiration date: "OCT 14 2014." Sighing, he called a clerk over.

"Good morning sir, may I help you?"

"Yes. Why is this juice not refrigerated?"

"Well, our refrigerators run on propane, and there's a propane shortage- "

"Because of the corn crop," they said together.

Darren asked, "What am I supposed to do with this?"

The clerk replied, "It should be good if you boil it for a few minutes."

"Boil the orange juice?"

"Yes sir."

"Wouldn't the citric acid corrode whatever pan I boil it in?"

"I mean just boil it in a mug in your microwave."

"Oh. Okay. Thanks." Darren walked away, leaving the juice behind. He walked casually through the neighborhood, taking note of the local churches in the area. Most of the churches had signage indicating the number of services they held each week. In spite of his casual inquiry, or perhaps because of it, Darren considered taking a break from ministry. He was tired from the months of doing his part to promote justice in food distribution. His desk job at the denomination's headquarters was a bore. All he wanted was to be in a community of faith and love... if such a community existed.

As he continued walking, he passed a small grocery store. Hearing the laughter of the people inside, he doubled back and went in. What he saw shocked him.

The shelves were full. There was milk, fresh fruit, unexpired canned goods, and bread. Music was playing.

With a stunned look on his face, he walked up to the cashier. "Excuse me, where did all this come from?"

The cashier laughed and extended his hand. "I have friends, man! Anything you want I can get it for you."

Darren looked around again as he shook hands. "I'm Darren," he said.

"I'm Mike," the cashier replied.

"Um, Mike, I don't see any prices posted."

"Right. The prices vary based on a number of factors. Availability, season, gas prices, delivery risk,-"

"Delivery risk?"

"Yeah. It costs more to deliver to the inner cities. Too many people, too many thieves, too many CFM agents. Suburbs are easier."

"But Mike, isn't this Boston?"

"Well, technically we're in Boston, but this ain't the inner city. How many times were you stopped?"

"Huh?"

"Darren, are you new to the area?"

"Yes, I am."

"Lemme give you a crash course." Mike pulled out a city map from behind the counter and grabbed a stubby pencil. "Okay." He drew a large circle around several blocks. "You see this? Don't go into this community for any reason. It's not safe." He then handed Darren the map. "Where are you staying?"

Darren squinted a bit at the tiny print, then pointed to an area northwest of the circle Mike had drawn.

"Okay Darren. That is a good place to be."

"But Mike, when I started walking, the stores I went into looked terrible."

Mike laughed. "Yeah, what a difference a block makes! It's like heaven owns one side and hell owns the other."

"Hmm," Darren mused. "Okay. I'm gonna keep walking. Is it all right if I- "

"Dude, you definitely need to keep the map! Don't go into that area I circled. Seriously."

"Thank you." Darren turned to leave, then went back. "Mike?"

"Yeah?"

"Do you have orange juice?"

Mike held up his hand as if to say "*Wait*," then ducked into the back of the store. He soon reappeared with a ten ounce bottle of cold orange juice. Darren glanced at the expiration date: FEB 12 2015.

"Mike, where did you get this?"

"I've got friends, that's all I can say."

"How much is it?"

"It's three dollars, but you don't pay this time. It's my gift to you."

"Thanks!" Darren put the small bottle in his jacket pocket.

"Enjoy it dude. It's nice every now and then to get something for free. But next time, you gotta pay. I can't give away the store."

"I understand. Take care Mike."

"You too man. Welcome to Boston!"

Chapter Eleven: November 2014

It was Thursday morning, November 27th. Renee had been awake for a few hours. Although there was a gas shortage, several companies donated money and personnel so that the Thanksgiving Day Parade could continue as planned. Renee watched on TV as the floats and balloons worked their way through midtown Manhattan. Several of the spectators were crying, anticipating that this would be the final year of the parade.

R-r-r-ing!

Renee absent-mindedly reached for her house phone, then realized it was her doorbell that rang. *"Who would be coming here today?"* she wondered silently. *"And how did they get into the building without ringing the intercom first? Is it the police?"*

Looking through the peephole, she saw a man with several bags, carrying an overcoat on his arm. His baseball cap and hooded sweatshirt bore one word: YALE.

"Ronald!" Renee opened the door. "Ronald, come in!" She quickly shut the door behind him.

"Hi Sis! Happy Thanksgiving!" Ronald put his coat and bags down and gave her a hug. "I could've left my coat at home. I had no idea the weather would be so nice."

"Ronald, I have to ask you something."

"Ask."

"I visited Gate Beautiful a couple of months ago and saw your picture. They called you 'Pastor Ronald'."

"That is not an 'ask'."

"Ronald, why didn't you tell me?"

He sighed. "I'm not sure why I didn't tell you. It just didn't seem … I mean, I'm ordained, but I'm not a pastor in the conventional sense."

"But we're friends."

"Renee, there's- yes, we're friends, you're right. But I haven't told you all I've done since we were in school together. Frankly, there's some things you don't need to know."

"Ronald, if I knew you were a minister I would have asked you some things."

"That's precisely my point." Ronald looked away for a moment. Then, he looked directly into Renee's eyes. "Sis, I'm realizing our relationship is changing."

"That's okay, isn't it? We're still friends. Is there such a difference with my knowing you're a minister?"

"That might be evidenced by what you ask me now that you would not have asked me nine months ago." Turning the conversation, Ronald kept talking. "You know, you haven't asked me why I'm in New York today."

Renee raised an eyebrow. "Does your presence mean that you're not at Yale anymore?"

"I'm still there," Ronald answered. "But I won't be there much longer."

"So why are you in New York?"

"Well, I figured the police would be busy with the parade and the CFM would be busy with their families, so they wouldn't be looking for me. And, I figured that you might not want to eat Thanksgiving dinner alone."

Renee, confused, looked at Ronald. After a few seconds she put words to her thoughts. "Are you saying you're risking getting arrested just to observe Thanksgiving with me?"

"Yes."

"Um, I see you have bags with you."

Ronald laughed. "I can't deny that a part of me wouldn't mind staying! But I have to go back to New Haven today. These bags are for you; I mean, I won't be back for a while, so this is sort of Thanksgiving and Christmas at the same time." He reached into one bag and pulled out two frozen dinners. "I've been on the road with these a few hours but they're still good."

Renee laughed in response. "These are perfect! We can eat on TV trays like our crew used to do in grad school." Suddenly, she stopped smiling. "Ronald, are we really just friends?"

He kept smiling. "It's okay. We're good friends, and we're just friends. Let's catch the rest of the parade."

"Okay."

"But we should talk after the parade."

Renee put the TV dinners into the oven, then returned to the living room. She and Ronald watched the parade, ate lunch while watching the football game, then started watching a second game. During the halftime show, Ronald spoke up.

"Renee, let's talk."

"TV?"

"It can stay on. I don't know if I'll be back in New York. I'd like to come back in February. But if I can't, I'll let you know. The rest of the food in the bags doesn't need refrigeration. That includes the milk."

"What?"

Ronald reached into the bag and pulled out a six-ounce carton of milk. "These are good for six months, no refrigeration. In case the county loses electricity or gas during the winter. Same for the juices: they're specially packaged to go unrefrigerated. Six months."

"Wow, that's cool, no refrigeration!" Renee laughed at her own wordplay. "I'll stock these in the linen closet next to the bathroom."

Ronald smiled. "And, before I forget, I've really been missing my little Bible verse paper."

"The box! I'll get it." Renee walked to the kitchen and pulled his jewelry box from a cabinet drawer. Bringing it back, she opened the box and handed it to him.

Ronald looked at her. "Oh, the I.O.U."

"It's okay," Renee replied. "I figured you had probably forgotten about it."

"Please open the side pocket of that bag."

She reached into the side pocket and pulled out a jewelry box. Though it was a different style and weight than Ronald's, it appeared to be large enough to hold a bracelet. She looked at him: he was no longer smiling. Neither was she.

"Ronald, I can't accept this."

"You haven't even opened it."

"This case looks expensive!"

"The case was free. Renee, please open it."

She opened the box and saw a leather bracelet. It was almost an inch wide. The outer band of the bracelet was engraved: MATTHEW 6:20. The inside band had the entire verse printed out.

"Ronald, this is beautiful."

"I want you to remember what really matters. Please keep it."

Renee kept staring at the bracelet. "I feel kind of weird about this."

"What's so odd about a friend giving a friend a Bible verse?"

"It's a bracelet."

"Please keep it. It's monogrammed."

She looked at the bracelet again, turning it around. "What monogram?"

Ronald picked up a pencil and pointed at the tiny set of letters under the scripture verse: R.L.D.

Renee sighed and shook her head. "This is a big deal."

"When I left my job in Chicago they gave me a five hundred dollar watch. And they weren't my friends."

Just then, Ronald's phone alarm sounded. He quickly shut it off. "Sis, I have to leave soon so I can catch the next New Haven train. You know they only run once every three hours on holidays."

"Okay. I'm glad you stopped by! Please be careful going back."

"I will." Ronald pulled off his hooded jacket and put it into his bag. Putting on his coat, he smiled once more. "Stay encouraged sis." He took the bracelet from her hand and put it on her wrist. "Please. You keep this." As he walked to the door, she followed him.

"Ronald? Were you going to pray?"

"Already done. I talked with God while I was talking with you." He gave her a quick hug. "Bye sis. Take care."

"Goodbye."

With a wave, he walked down the block and turned the corner. Renee walked back into the apartment and glanced at the bracelet again.

"God? Thank you. God? Why does his good-bye always feel like a permanent good-bye?"

Silence.

Chapter Twelve: December 2014

Darren glanced at the caller I.D. on his office phone: 607. He picked up the receiver. "Hello?"

"Hi Darren, it's Mike."

"Mike from the store?"

"Yeah. I got a delivery of some new things, and I figured since you're a good customer I'd let you be one of the first to check it out."

"Thanks, but I'll have to take a raincheck. I need to pick up a friend of mine from the airport, and with the weather I'm not sure when his plane will be allowed to land."

"No problem dude. Another time then."

"Mike, why does my caller I.D. say you're calling from Ithaca?"

"Huh?"

"607. That area code is for Ithaca. New York."

"Yeah, yeah. I got a great deal on this new phone from a friend of mine. Ithaca, Peoria, same difference. All I care about is the dial tone. I'm here in my store."

"Okay. See you another time."

"Yeah." Mike hung up.

Darren hung up the receiver and put on his coat. It was almost five o'clock, and he wanted to get to the airport before the evening rush hour.

On the road, his thoughts turned to Gate Beautiful. It was the Advent season, and he sorely missed his days of planning services. *"Oh well, I guess headquarters is enough of a parish,"* he thought to himself.

After a two hour delay, the plane landed safely. Darren stood behind a partition opposite the baggage claim area.

"Darren?"

Darren turned. "Ronald!" They gave each other a handshake as he continued. "Shouldn't you still be on the other side of this partition? How did you get through without going through the baggage claim?"

"Old ninja trick," Ronald laughed.

"Very funny. You're no ninja." Darren glanced up at the clock. "Let's get on the road; the weather is supposed to get worse through the night."

"Okay."

At the rectory, Ronald and Darren stood talking in the kitchen.

"How's the Boston life treating you?" Ronald asked.

Darren smiled. "It seems the denomination's punishment of me isn't working. I'm starting to like being here. I miss my old job, but I've found other tasks to keep me occupied. By the way, I made a new contact that you should meet."

Ronald didn't answer right away. He found a mug and filled it with water. Placing it in the microwave, he turned back to Darren. "My friend, I've been thinking about passing this baton to someone else."

Darren responded quickly. "You're kidding. You're the best we have."

"I'm flattered," Ronald replied. "But let me point out a few things. I'm old. I'm tired. And if I stay too long I might become more of a liability than an asset."

"How old are you?"

"Thirty-nine, going on sixty."

"That's not old!"

"Darren, man, I can't run like I used to. I've lost my edge."

"You had no problem bypassing the baggage claim!"

Ronald smiled. "I'll teach you how to do that."

Darren shook his head. "No, no! I don't do national work. I'm staying right here." Remembering Renee, he changed the subject. "Whatever happened to your friend? Renee?"

"She's still in Kings County."

"How's her situation?"

"I took her some food on Thanksgiving. She's good through January or so."

"Nice."

"And I bought her a leather bracelet."

"You *what*?"

"I-"

"I heard you! What did she say?"

"She said she felt uncomfortable keeping it."

"So you took it back."

"No. I kept pressing until she kept it."

"So she's a little more than a friend then."

"No Darren. I care about her but not like that."

"Are you kidding? Leather costs more than gold nowadays."

"I know, believe me. I paid two hundred bucks to have it custom-made."

"Are you in denial or something?"

"You want me to say I love her." Ronald put his mug of water, still tepid, back into the microwave. "Fine. I love her. But really, she's like my sister."

"Uh-huh. Is your 'sister' as sweet as that hot chocolate you're making?" Darren laughed and ducked as Ronald threw a plastic spoon at him.

Ronald protested, "I'm serious! You just wait and watch. Time will vindicate me."

"Maybe you should have bought her a watch then."

Chapter Thirteen: January 2015

C-c-c-crash!

"SHHH!"

Renee woke up, jolted by the sound of shattering glass. She sat up in bed… and then, she heard the voices.

"Man, this fridge is almost empty."

"How can the refrigerator be empty? I'm telling you, this place gets Elite Fleet deliveries every month. There's got to be food here."

Renee slid out from beneath the covers and crawled under her bed.

"Check the cupboards." The two men combed through the nearly empty kitchen pantry.

"Tuna. Crackers." They grabbed the food and put it in a knapsack.

"Let's get out of here."

"No, there's got to be more somewhere. I'm telling you, Elite Fleet-"

"No. I'm telling you, 'empty shelves'! Time to go."

The two men left through her front door and ran out of the apartment building, glancing to their left and right. Then, one looked up.

"CFM camera!"

"Did you set me up?!?" The other man grabbed his associate by the jacket and started shaking him. "You set me up?!?"

"Man, honest, I didn't know!"

They soon stopped scuffling with each other and ran, but their seconds of arguing added enough time for the police cars to arrive. Seeing five officers with guns drawn, the two thieves stopped running and held their hands high in surrender. By this time Renee had come to the building entrance, shaking in the cold. One of the officers walked over to her.

"Miss, are you all right? I'll need to take a statement from you."

"Yes sir."

"May we step back inside? It's cold and you're not dressed for the weather."

"Yes sir."

"Did they hurt you?"

"No, I, they didn't see me. I was hiding under my bed."

It took nearly half an hour for the officer to interview Renee and complete his report. "Miss Dupree, is there anything else you would like to add?"

"No sir."

"Okay." The officer tapped a button on his micropad. "I just sent in the report. There's nothing else you'll need to do."

"Will I have to go to court?"

"No, it's all taken care of. Your residence is already listed as an O.S.B. so this will be an easy conviction."

"O.S.B.?" Renee asked.

"You have an out-of-state benefactor, or at least we assume you do, based on the frequency of the Elite Fleet deliveries you've received versus the number of orders you've personally placed by mail or over the Internet." Renee's face began to get hot as the officer continued speaking. "Those thieves aren't the only ones watching who gets what and how they get it."

He then shut off his micropad and spoke in a low voice. "Miss Dupree, my mother lives in this county. I've been sending her food using Elite Fleet as well."

Tears started to roll down Renee's face. The officer kept talking. "Miss Dupree, I'm taking a week off to move my mom to the suburbs. I suggest you contact whoever is helping you and find a way to get out of here. The city is going to explode soon and we don't have enough police to manage the chaos."

As he headed toward the door he spoke again. "It seems odd to say, but I do hope you'll have a happy new year, in spite of the challenges."

Renee remained in the entryway for a few minutes: shaking from the incident, shivering from the cold, and sobbing. After the police car disappeared down the block, she went back into her apartment. Bypassing the kitchen, she walked down the hallway and opened the linen closet that was next to the bathroom. Her tears of sadness mixed with tears of joy, grateful that she had never moved Ronald's Thanksgiving delivery into the kitchen.

She retrieved a whisk broom and dustpan from the lowest shelf and went back to the front of the apartment. In a few minutes, she had swept up the broken glass and taped plastic bags and cardboard over the window the thieves had broken.

Sitting in her living room, she picked up her phone. It was nearly three o'clock in the morning. *"Who can I call at this hour?"* she wondered, then answered herself aloud. "No one. I can handle this on my own."

She turned on her television. To her surprise, she saw Cathy on the screen.

"If a thousand of us, if five thousand of us, if ten thousand of us band together, the CFM will have to take notice!"

A cheer rose from the crowd as Cathy continued.

"Is it fair that Manhattan, the center of the world, is subjected to substandard food?"

"No!" the crowd shouted.

"Is it fair for us to be stopped and searched because we are trying to feed our families?"

"No!"

"Is it fair to distribute AC-cess bracelets to some, but not to all?"

"No!"

"Is it fair for affluent people to get food delivered to their doorstep while the community's poor are starving?"

"No!"

Renee stood up, shocked. *"How could Cathy say such a thing knowing that she herself was a beneficiary of my having food sent from out-of-state?"* Suddenly, Renee felt an overwhelming sense of danger.

"This," Cathy continued, "This month, January 2015, marks a turn for us. We are turning back to our glory days of protest! We are turning back to our glory days of standing up and defending our rights!"

A cheer came up from the crowd.

"This is our Berlin Wall! This is our square!"

"Oh no," Renee thought. *"Cathy's starting a riot."*

The news commentator cut in with a voice-over. "Ladies and gentlemen, what you've been hearing is one of several speakers who have addressed a crowd of, it appears to be about thirty thousand people and growing, who have assembled in Central Park for what they are calling the New Year's Protest. This protest appears to have been organized through various social media outlets. As far as we can tell, the crowd is a mixture of both local county residents and persons who have come in from the other counties which comprise New York City. At present, the protestors are all in Central Park and there have been no reports of rioting. However, we have received word that the management of Price-Rite Supermarkets will close all of their New York City locations as a precautionary measure, and will re-open when they have employed additional security guards. We now take you back to the audio of this protest, a curious beginning to 2015."

Renee picked up her cell phone and dialed the number she had promised herself she wouldn't call. Ronald answered on the second ring.

"Sis, if you're calling me at this hour it must be an emergency."

"My apartment was broken into and Cathy is starting a riot!"

"Are you all right?"

"Yes, the police came."

"Cathy is rioting outside of your apartment?"

"No, no."

"Sis, take a deep breath. Help me understand."

"My apartment was broken into around one-thirty this morning but the cops came right away."

"Got it."

"I turned on the TV a few minutes ago and there's a rally going on right now in Central Park.

Cathy told the people to take back their county." Renee started crying.

"Do you need me to come down there?"

"One of the officers told me they don't have enough personnel to deal with this. I'm sorry, you were the first person I thought of. I understand if there's nothing you can do."

"I'll come and get you." Ronald got up and started pulling clothing out of his suitcase. "Try not to leave the apartment unless it's an emergency. I'll be there in five hours, okay?"

"Okay."

"Hang up. I'll see you soon."

"Okay." Renee ended the call, then went to her bedroom to pack a small bag.

Ronald knocked on Darren's bedroom door. "Darren! Darren!" Not waiting for a response, Ronald opened the door.

Darren, half-awake, frowned. "Man, are you kidding?"

"I need to borrow your car so that I can get Renee out of New York City today. This can't wait."

Darren, sensing the urgency in Ronald's voice, got up. "I'll go with you. I know some back roads that'll cut down the drive time."

On the drive from Boston, the men stayed quiet for the first several minutes. Then Ronald spoke.

"My friend, would you be willing to receive my confession?"

"Yes. I absolve you."

"You can't absolve me. I haven't confessed yet!"

"I absolve you for waking me up at such an ungodly hour," Darren laughed.

Ronald went on. "It's about Renee. I care for her deeply."

"I know that already."

"I want to be her Guardian. Officially."

"Ronald, you know you can't do that. You don't have a pastorate. And, she already has a pastor."

"Her pastor is not standing guard over her soul."

Darren kept his eyes on the road. "Ronald, we're human beings with limitations. You can't go grabbing every sheep whose shepherd is a little lax."

"Darren, what if Renee was your sister?"

91

"Of course I'd guard my sister if she wasn't being covered by-"

"-someone else," they said together.

"But Ronald, you're not a pastor."

"I still hold an office though." Ronald looked out of the window, then looked back at Darren. "You know I'm not like this. This is a special case."

"Are you sure it's not love?"

"I would love to see her in better spiritual shape than she is."

"A love that turns you into a thief?"

"I guess I'm really a smuggler now, huh?" Ronald covered his face with his hands. "God, help me."

"Maybe we should ask Renee what *she* wants."

Ronald glanced at his watch. "We should be there soon. Thanks for driving."

"Sure. And by the way, I'm aware that you haven't answered my questions. But I absolve you anyway, and I pray I won't suffer for it."

Three hours later, they were in Westchester County. The skies were still dark. Darren turned into the parking lot at the county airport. Ronald hopped out of the car, left the parking lot, passed by the taxi stand, and walked to the bus stop. A few minutes later, he boarded an express bus bound for Kings County.

The bus moved quickly, the advantage of traveling early in the day. An hour later, Ronald was off the bus and walking towards Renee's apartment. Though he was concerned about the security cameras, he kept walking and was about to turn the corner onto her block. Suddenly, he remembered his cell phone. He stopped on the corner and called. "Renee?"

"Yes Ronald?"

"I'm here at the corner."

"Yes, I'll be right there."

As she neared him, he took her bag. "We have to hurry," he said. "It'll be daylight soon."

They walked a few blocks, and waited in silence for the bus that would take them back north. By the time their bus reached the Westchester County Airport, the skies were bright. The airport was nearly empty. Ronald led Renee to the food court on the lower level.

"We'll stay here until the next flight comes in, so that we can leave with the commuting crowd-there should be a few travelers passing through."

"Can I treat you to a hot chocolate?" Renee asked.

"Only if I can treat you to a cup of tea."

"Fair deal," Renee replied.

As they sat and waited for the next flight to arrive, Ronald decided to take Darren's counsel. "Renee, there's something I want to do for you but I need to ask your permission."

"What?"

"You've been going to church a long time, but you really don't know too much about your faith. I want to help you grow up."

"But I grew up in the church. How can you say I don't know too much?"

"Sis, I know that you know church. But I'm not sure that you know Christ." A low din of noise caught Ronald's attention. "Let's go: the flight's early." They got up and merged into the crowd of arriving passengers.

After a few minutes, they were outside with a few dozen people heading towards the parking lot. Once they were safely in Darren's car, they drove past the payment gate. A sign was in the window:

"It's always nice to get something for free…
FREE PARKING January 1st through 7th. Happy
New Year!"

Darren and Ronald, both seated in front of the car, talked. Renee, tired from having been awake most of the night, slept in the back.

"Renee?" Darren's voice broke through her reverie.

"Mm?"

"We're at a rest stop."

"Oh, okay, thanks." She got out of the car and headed for the restroom.

Ronald and Darren meandered through the food court. All the smaller items were on shelves behind the cashier: gum, candy, cigarettes. The racks that used to hold bags of pretzels and potato chips were empty.

After a few minutes, Renee found the men at the pizza stand. Darren, noticing the expression on her face, glanced at Ronald.

"Did you two ever finish your conversation?"

Ronald answered. "It's unfinished."

Renee added, "I think I understand what Ronald was saying."

"Well," Darren answered, "we want you to know even more than what we know. In a normal situation I would not advise you and Ronald to do this. But maybe this current crisis is an opportunity for God to teach you more about Himself. And I can guarantee you that Ronald is one of the best Bible teachers I know."

Ronald added, "And God needs people like you to carry on the work."

"You talk like you won't be around," Renee said, frowning.

"I can't say one way or the other. But either way, you still need to know more than you do."

The trio walked back to the car. A short while later, they arrived at Elm Street. As they entered Ronald's apartment, Renee paused just inside the door. "Am I staying here?"

"Short-term. Until things cool down in the city. I'm headed back to Boston with Darren, so you'll have the place to yourself." Seeing Renee's sadness, Ronald turned to Darren and said, "But maybe I can go back in a day or two…"

Darren nodded. "I think it might be better if she's not left alone today."

"I'd appreciate that," Renee added.

"Okay, I'm headed back up the road." Darren put his hat and gloves back on. He nodded to Ronald. "Boss."

"Yes. We'll talk."

Ronald locked the door behind Darren. "You should rest," he said to Renee.

"No, I'd like to get started with this study thing."

"Okay. You'll need your Bible."

"I don't have one."

"You left it behind?"

"No. I don't have one at all."

Ronald reached and retrieved a Bible from one of his bookshelves. "You can have this one." He quickly crossed out his name and wrote hers.

"Thanks! Do we start at Genesis?"

"Let's start with John."

Chapter Fourteen: February 2015

"This has got to be against the law! I've been here forty days." Cathy stood in a cell with over thirty people, with barely enough room to raise an arm. A young man responded to her comment.

"No, it's the law. We can be held here indefinitely."

"When was that law passed?"

"I don't know when it was passed, but I have a friend who was detained in Chicago for six months, back in 2013."

"That's crazy. I was only detained for twenty days last time."

"You wanna hear crazy? My friend was never even charged with anything."

Their conversation was interrupted by a man who appeared to be several years older than they.

"Hi, I'm Lucas. I'm trying to organize a demonstration."

Cathy and the young man looked at him, incredulous.

"Miss," Lucas continued, "during your speech in the park you said something like 'They can't stop all of us.' So, I figure that if we can get a mob together to draw attention to our situation, we should all be able to get out."

"That is true," the young man replied.

"But how?" asked Cathy.

Lucas smiled. "I still have my phone and it still works. I was thinking we could each send notices over social media and have a huge mob form outside to help us get out." He pulled out his smartphone and showed them the back. "See? Solar panel."

"Wow," exclaimed Cathy, "I heard the solar phones were coming but I didn't know they were in New York already."

"They aren't," answered Lucas. "I picked this up at a little shop in Boston."

The trio admired the technology, oblivious to the tiny blinking light on the edge of the panel.

Chapter Fifteen: March 2015

"Renee?"

"I'll be right there." Renee closed her Bible and notebook and walked into the kitchen. Ronald handed her a cup of tea.

"Wow, you made me tea?"

"I have news to share. Let's go sit in the living room." Ronald paused for a long while. "The CFM has partnered with a military unit that's been specially assigned to the downstate counties of New York. It's very safe for you to go back home. There's tons of security."

"Oh!" Renee exclaimed, then she repeated herself more soberly. "Oh."

"Sis, I can't go back into New York. It's too risky. I can't compromise the few contacts I have there."

"I know... you're saying I won't see you anymore."

"Sis-" Ronald stopped and looked down, suddenly conscious of the emotion in his voice. Renee looked away as he continued. "Sis, you have the basics of the faith. There's other things to know, but I can't teach them to you. You have to grow into them."

"Ronald, I-" She turned to look at him. He looked up. Seeing tears in her eyes brought tears to his own. He got up and walked over to her chair.

"Sis, what can I do?"

"Nothing. But I don't understand how I love you, but I don't love you. That doesn't make sense."

"It makes perfect sense. It's *agape*."

"The love that comes from God?"

"Right! And I'm so glad you love me that way. You're so beautiful."

"You too. I mean, handsome. Whatever. This is so weird!" She laughed, but Ronald didn't.

"Sis, I need to tell you some very bad news."

"About you?"

"No. About your friend Cathy."

"I haven't heard from her since that New Year's Protest rally a couple of months ago, except for something she posted about another mob event."

Ronald pulled up a chair and sat next to Renee.

"Ronald, is she sick?" Renee felt a sense of dread rising as he spoke.

"Cathy was detained right after the New Year's Protest. She apparently got involved in a plot to incite another riot or something. But, what happened was that the mob stormed into the detention center. When they came in, the guards just started firing on everyone. They were supposed to be using pepper spray, but instead they broke out with live artillery." Ronald stopped, sighing and putting his head in his hands. "Sis, Cathy was still in the holding cell. There was nowhere for her to run."

"They killed her?"

"One of the bullets hit her. She was taken to the hospital but she didn't make it."

"Are you sure?"

"Yes. My friend Ryan is conducting her funeral after the internal affairs investigation is completed." As Renee's shock turned into a flood of tears, Ronald put his arms around her. "I'm so sorry, sis."

After a while, Renee was able to speak. "It hurts so much losing her. And you."

"Yes. I know how you feel. This won't be easy. But I promise you God will help you through."

"I know you can't come to New York right away, but maybe when things get better?"

"No, sis. The New York run is done. I know I won't be back." Ronald took Renee's tea mug and headed to the kitchen. As he finished pouring the tea down the drain, he turned to see her standing next to him.

"I think I should be at Cathy's funeral."

"Yes. I'll connect you with Ryan."

"Thank you for teaching me these past two months, and for getting me a proper winter coat and boots. I'll really miss you."

"I'll miss you too. Oh, there's one more thing." Ronald went back into the living room and brought a small package into the kitchen.

"Is this another bracelet?"

"Do you want me to answer, or should you just open the box?" Before Renee could respond, Ronald said, "Yes, it's a bracelet. But I want you to open the box and take a look."

She opened the box and pulled out a silver-colored AC-cess bracelet. "Ronald, thank you!"

"I know you're concerned about your neighbors. This is an F-5 bracelet, the same kind used by itinerant emergency workers. It's valid in any county within a five-state range, and you have no limit on purchases."

"Five states?"

"Yes. New York, New Jersey, Connecticut, and also Pennsylvania and Massachusetts. But look in the box again."

Renee pulled out a plastic card. "AmeriCash?"

"Whenever you go to a supermarket, just use this card to pay for whatever you need. I have a couple of contacts taking care of the cost. Until we have a better way, at least this is a beginning for you to bless your community."

She gave him a hug, trying not to cry again. He held her tightly. "Sis, it's just us. I don't mind if you cry."

Chapter Sixteen: April 2015

As Renee slept on her living room sofa, the television news continued to sound throughout the apartment.

"Earlier today, Cathy Walsh was laid to rest. Her funeral, conducted by megachurch pastor Ryan Kashir, was held at the Hundredfold Worship Center in lower Manhattan. A number of attendees sympathetic to the riot movement wore red jackets in protest of the detainment policy that was a contributing factor in Cathy's demise.

"The sentiment of the service was made clear in the words of county resident Renee Dupree, a childhood friend of Cathy's who is not part of the protest movement." The television flashed a sound bite, Renee's face looking drained against her black suit and hat. "This is the event no parent, no friend, no person wants to attend. But attend we must. We attend because we all know the value of mutual respect and the utter necessity of justice for all. Cathy, I am not in a position to give you the justice that is due you. But I can certainly pay you respect." The picture flashed back to the news correspondent.

"So, after a lengthy investigation, Cathy Walsh finally rests in peace. But whether peace will come for others in the movement remains to be seen. This is Jan West, reporting for Kings County News."

Hours later, Renee's alarm clock sounded. She got up and walked to the kitchen, almost tripping over her own feet. As she pulled a teabag out of its container, she began speaking aloud.

"God, I wish You would talk to me like You talk to Ronald."

Silence.

"He told me he hears You. All I hear are birds and traffic."

Silence.

Renee sighed as she poured hot water into her tea mug. A thought came to her: *"Maybe I should read the Bible."* She went to her bedroom and got her Bible, stopped back in the kitchen for her tea, and took both into the living room. Turning off the television, she began to read.

Into your hand I entrust my life; you will rescue me, O Lord, the faithful God. I hate those who serve worthless idols, but I trust in the Lord. I will be happy and rejoice in your faithfulness, because you notice my pain and you are aware of how distressed I am. You do not deliver me over to the power of the enemy; you enable me to stand in a wide open place.

Renee smiled. *"Ah, Lord, now I hear You!"*

*****

Darren noticed the squad cars when he was still two blocks away from Mike's store. Not sure whether to keep walking forward or make a U-turn, he opted to walk one more block. Making a right turn at the corner, he saw two of Mike's employees conversing with uniformed officers. Darren walked down the block, made a second right turn, and gave Mike a call.

"Darren! Is this another 'come-to-church-with-me' call? I know Easter is coming."

"Uh, no. Mike, I saw some law enforcement guys near your store. Is everything okay?"

"Sure, everything's cool. They're friends of mine."

"Oh. Okay."

"Stop by later, I got free samples of jellybeans."

"Sure, I'll try to stop by. It's nice to get a freebie every now and then."

"All right Darren." As Mike ended the call, his phone rang again.

"Mike here."

"Mike, Ronald."

"I know a lot of Ronalds."

"Sorry- I'm a friend of Darren's."

"Oh, *that* Ronald! At last we get to connect. I got some good-looking goods that I know will be good for you." As Mike rattled off his inventory, Ronald noticed that Darren was calling. *"I'll call him back later,"* Ronald thought to himself.

"Mike, sounds great. I'm kind of tied up with other things but I'll do my best to stop by next month."

"Next month? You'll miss the Easter sale!"

"Wow, yeah. Too bad I'll miss it. Take care."

"Yeah. You too." Mike hung up and turned to one of his officer friends. "Dave, are you sure this fish is worth catching? He seems pretty low-level to me."

Officer Dave smiled. "Things aren't always as they seem."

Chapter Seventeen: May 2015

"Are you sure? My budget isn't big enough for cross-country wild goose chases." The Chicago liaison for the Council for Famine Management shook his head. "I need something solid, Aaron."

"Well, I'll tell you what. You know I had a meeting about a year ago with Blake Stearns. He's still your boss, right?"

"Yeah."

"Ronald Lee's been on the East Coast since then. We're very close to reining him in."

The Chicago liaison sighed audibly. "I hope you'll pardon my lack of enthusiasm, but I've heard this story before."

"This is my last year as City Commissioner and I can assure you that before my year is up Reverend Lee will be in your backyard, not mine."

"All right, Aaron. Let me ask you a small favor. When you catch him, have one of the Boston guys drive him here with one of my guys."

"I can't have officers driving across state lines!"

"Then fly him here. There's nothing specific in the manual about extradition by air."

Aaron paused and considered the request. "I'll let you know whether it's a fly or a drive."

"Great. Call me as soon as you know."

*****

"Ronald, you should stay put." Darren paced the floor. His voice was barely above a whisper, as if he was concerned about being overheard.

"Mike is not a problem," Ronald answered.

"But I've been living here eight months and I've never seen or heard about these guys until last month."

"God's got my back."

"I hope you're right."

Ronald laughed. " 'Hope'? Where's your faith?"

"Apparently it's not where yours is."

"Darren, if these guys are so sharp then why aren't they parked here outside of your office?"

"I don't know. I don't know."

"Maybe this is it for me."

"I wish you wouldn't talk like that."

Ronald started to move towards the door. "I told you six months ago that it's about time for me to move on. I don't know where I'll end up. But I know I have to go to Mike's store today."

Darren shook Ronald's hand. "Well, I've been behind a desk for a while, but I do remember what it feels like when God is pressing us to do something. Take care. I'll be praying."

Ronald walked down the block; Darren returned to pacing the floor, his simple prayer ascending in whispers.

Eventually, Ronald reached the store. Mike was waiting near the front entrance, his arms full of *GoPicnic* snack boxes.

"Hey Ronald! Look what I got."

"Wow, how interesting. I haven't seen GoPicnic since..." Ronald paused and looked at Mike, then continued speaking. "I haven't seen these since I used to work in Chicago." Ronald was no longer smiling, and neither was Mike.

"Ronald, two men came here looking for you. One was a police officer from Chicago South. The other was a police officer from Boston North."

"To take me back to Chicago?"

"Yeah."

"Where are they now?"

"I sent them on a wild goose chase. They're on their way to New Haven." Seeing the confused look on Ronald's face, Mike continued speaking. "Look. The way I figure it, we're both doing the same thing. We get goods where they need to be. We provide service to our constituents. The only difference is that I keep an eye out for the well-to-do, and you keep an eye out for the disenfranchised. I respect that."

"Mike, why?"

"I'm just freeing you up so that you can get your work done. It's always good to get a free pass, right?" Without waiting for Ronald to answer, Mike added, "Speaking of free, the Easter Bunny left you something. Follow me."

Mike took the lead and Ronald followed as they walked through the store and exited out of the back. Walking into the small parking lot, Mike turned to Ronald. "You drive, right?"

"Yes, I do."

"Bike?"

"I have a bicycle but I left it with a friend."

"No, a bike. Motorcycle."

"It's been a while, but yes."

Mike handed Ronald two keys and pointed to a motorcycle at the end of the lot. "She's got a few miles on her, but still a lot of good miles left." Mike smiled. "Just like us."

Ronald smiled and took the keys. "I guess we'll both be working a little bit longer."

"Yeah." The two men shook hands. "Ronald, I respect you. You're putting yourself on the line for no profit at all."

"No, Mike. I'm getting a huge profit in this venture. It's not monetary, but I'm really wealthy." Ronald reached into his pocket and pulled out the old jewelry case he'd carried for so many years. "Mike, here's your freebie."

Mike opened the case. "A piece of paper?"

"It's a little Bible verse that's kept me going strong for a long time. You keep it. Oh, wait a second." Ronald took out a pen and wrote something else on the paper. "Okay. You have a Bible?"

"I have them in the store. I can treat myself to one." They shook hands again, and Mike stood and waved as Ronald rode out of the parking lot.

As Ronald disappeared out of view, Mike unfolded the paper:

MATTHEW 6:20-34. *Mike, you've taken care of lots of people. Why not let God take care of you?* –R.

After thinking about the note for a few seconds, Mike called to one of his employees. "Can you bring me one of those Bibles from Aisle Three? I'm gonna hang out in the parking lot during lunch and do a little reading."

b'day card Beth
Lumity-eye

Made in the USA
Middletown, DE
04 February 2024

49072720R10066